Y
Picture
ISA

For Sue and Curly

NANCY PAULSEN BOOKS
An imprint of Penguin Young Readers Group
Published by The Penguin Group
Penguin Group (USA) Inc., 375 Hudson Street, New York, NY 10014, USA

USA | Canada | UK | Ireland | Australia | New Zealand | India | South Africa | China
Penguin Books Ltd, Registered Offices: 80 Strand, London WC2R 0RL, England
For more information about the Penguin Group, visit penguin.com

Library of Congress Cataloging-in-Publication Data is available upon request.

Published simultaneously in Canada. Manufactured in China by South China Printing Co. Ltd.
ISBN 978-0-399-25740-7
1 3 5 7 9 10 8 6 4 2

Design by Marikka Tamura.
Text set in Geist.
The illustrations were done with oil paints, printed paper, palette paper, ink and pencil.
The publisher does not have any control over and does not assume any responsibility for author or third-party websites or their content.

ALWAYS LEARNING   PEARSON

OLD MIKAMBA HAD A FARM

RACHEL ISADORA

NANCY PAULSEN BOOKS ✪ AN IMPRINT OF PENGUIN GROUP (USA) INC.

OLD MIKAMBA HAD A FARM
E-I-E-I-O

And on this farm he had a **BABOON**

E-I-E-I-O

With an

OOH-HA-HA here

And an

OOH-HA-HA there

Here an **OOH**, there an **OOH**
Everywhere an **OOH-HA-HA**

OLD MIKAMBA HAD A FARM E-I-E-I-O

And on this farm he had an **ELEPHANT**

E-I-E-I-O

With a

BARAAA-BARAAA here

And a

BARAAA-BARAAA there

Here a **BARAAA**, there a **BARAAA**
Everywhere a **BARAAA-BARAAA**

OLD MIKAMBA HAD A FARM E-I-E-I-O

And on this farm he had a **ZEBRA**
E-I-E-I-O

With a
WHINNY-WHINNY here

And a
WHINNY-WHINNY there

Here a **WHINNY**, there a **WHINNY**
Everywhere a **WHINNY-WHINNY**

OLD MIKAMBA HAD A FARM **E-I-E-I-O**

And on this farm he had a **CHEETAH**
E-I-E-I-O

With a
GRRRR-GRRRR here

And a
GRRRR-GRRRR there

Here a **GRRRR**, there a **GRRRR**
Everywhere a **GRRRR-GRRRR**

OLD MIKAMBA HAD A FARM E-I-E-I-O

And on this farm he had a **DASSIE**

E-I-E-I-O

With a
TRILL-TRILL here

And a
TRILL-TRILL there

Here a **TRILL**, there a **TRILL**
Everywhere a **TRILL-TRILL**

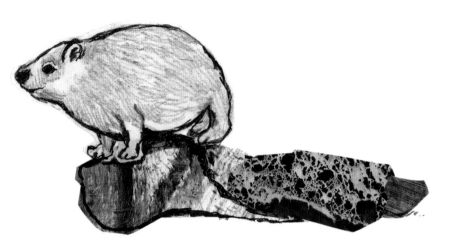

OLD MIKAMBA HAD A FARM E-I-E-I-O

And on this farm he had a **WARTHOG**
E-I-E-I-O

With a **SNORT-SNORT** here

And a **SNORT-SNORT** there

Here a **SNORT**,
there a **SNORT**
Everywhere a **SNORT-SNORT**

OLD MIKAMBA HAD A FARM E-I-E-I-O

And on this farm he had a **HIPPO**
E-I-E-I-O

With a
GRUNT-GRUNT here

And a
GRUNT-GRUNT there

Here a **GRUNT**, there a **GRUNT**

Everywhere a **GRUNT-GRUNT**

OLD MIKAMBA HAD A FARM E-I-E-I-O

And on this farm he had a **GIRAFFE**

E-I-E-I-O

With a
BLEAT-BLEAT here

And a
BLEAT-BLEAT there

Here a **BLEAT**,
there a **BLEAT**
Everywhere a **BLEAT-BLEAT**

OLD MIKAMBA HAD A FARM
E-I-E-I-O

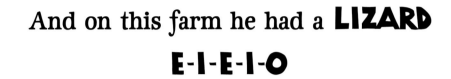

And on this farm he had a **LIZARD**
E-I-E-I-O

With a **HISS-HISS** here
And a **HISS-HISS** there

Here a **HISS**, there a **HISS**
Everywhere a **HISS-HISS**

OLD MIKAMBA HAD A FARM E-I-E-I-O

And on this farm he had a **SPRINGBOK**
E-I-E-I-O

With an
AH-AH-AH here

And an
AH-AH-AH there

Here an **AH**, there an **AH**
Everywhere an **AH-AH-AH**

OLD MIKAMBA HAD A FARM E-I-E-I-O

And on this farm he had a **PARROT**
E-I-E-I-O

With a
SQUAWK-SQUAWK here

And a
SQUAWK-SQUAWK there

Here a **SQUAWK,** there a **SQUAWK**
Everywhere a **SQUAWK-SQUAWK**

OLD MIKAMBA HAD A FARM E-I-E-I-O

And on this farm he had an **OSTRICH**
E-I-E-I-O

With a
CHIRP-CHIRP here

And a
CHIRP-CHIRP there

Here a **CHIRP**, there a **CHIRP**
Everywhere a **CHIRP-CHIRP**

OLD MIKAMBA HAD A FARM E-I-E-I-O

And on this farm he had a **RHINO**

E-I-E-I-O

With a **BELLOW-BELLOW** here

And a **BELLOW-BELLOW** there

Here a **BELLOW**, there a **BELLOW**
Everywhere a **BELLOW-BELLOW**

OLD MIKAMBA HAD A FARM E-I-E-I-O

And on this farm he had a **LION**

E-I-E-I-O

With a

ROAR-ROAR here

And a

ROAR-ROAR there

Here a **ROAR**, there a **ROAR**
Everywhere a **ROAR-ROAR**

OLD MIKAMBA HAD A FARM E-I-E-I-O

In Africa, you can see the greatest variety and number of wild animals and birds. Sadly, many of them are on the list of endangered species. Game farms and parks in Africa help save these amazing creatures from extinction. Here are some interesting facts about the ones in this book.

BABOON

Baboons are extremely social creatures and they use many different sounds to communicate with one another, ranging from grunts to barks to screams.

ELEPHANT

The elephant is the largest land animal, weighs about 200 pounds at birth, and grows to weigh between 10,000 and 13,000 pounds.

ZEBRA

The zebra belongs to the horse family and can run about 35 miles per hour. No two zebras have the same pattern of stripes.

CHEETAH

The cheetah is the fastest land animal in the world and can sprint up to 70 miles per hour. Unlike other big cats that roar, it gently purrs and chirps to communicate with other cheetahs.

DASSIE

The dassie is also known as the rock hyrax or rock rabbit because it lives among rocks and boulders. These small animals live in groups and communicate with one another using squeals, shrieks, whistles, and growls.

WARTHOG

The warthog is a wild African pig that has a mane like a horse and tusks that are used for fighting and digging. It has a large head with protruding wart-like bumps.

HIPPOPOTAMUS

The name hippopotamus means "river horse." The hippopotamus's nostrils, ears, and eyes are on the top of its head and stay above the water while the rest of it is beneath the surface. That way, a hippo can breathe, see, and hear even while its body is submerged.

GIRAFFE

The giraffe is the world's tallest land animal and stands around 18 feet high. Not only does it have a long neck, but it also has a tongue that is about 20 inches long.

FLAT LIZARD

These agile lizards perform acrobatic flips to catch the black flies that are a main part of their diet. The males are brightly colored to attract females; however, this also makes them more easily spotted by birds and other enemies.

SPRINGBOK

The springbok gets its name from its habit of leaping up to 10 feet in the air. They are extremely fast and can reach speeds of approximately 60 miles per hour.

PARROT

There are more than 370 species of parrots and they are considered some of the most intelligent of the bird species. Some parrots can live to be 80 years old.

OSTRICH

The ostrich is the largest bird at nine feet tall and about 350 pounds. While it is a bird and has wings and feathers, it does not fly . . . it runs—at speeds up to 40 miles per hour.

RHINOCEROS

The name rhinoceros means "nose horn." The rhinoceros is the second largest land mammal and can weigh over 7,700 pounds. When it catches the scent of a human or an unfamiliar creature, it is likely to charge.

LION

Lions live in groups known as prides. They roar to keep in touch with one another, and their roar is so loud, it can be heard up to five miles away.